The Cuddle Book • Copyright © 2003 Uitgeverij Clavis, Amsterdam - Hasselt • Printed in Italy. • All rights reserved. No part of this book may be used or reproduced in any manner whatsoever without written permission except in the case of brief quotations embodied in critical articles and reviews. • For information address HarperCollins Children's Books, a division of HarperCollins Publishers, 1350 Avenue of the Americas, New York, NY 10019. • www.harperchildrens.com • Library of Congress Cataloging-in-Publication Data • Genechten, Guido van • The cuddle book / by Guido van Genechten.— 1st U.S. ed. • p. cm. • First published in the Netherlands by Clavis Editions, 2003. • Summary: Describes a variety of animal cuddles, from bear hugs to porcupine hugs, but the best is Mommy's cuddle. • ISBN 0-06-075306-4 • [1. Mother and child—Fiction. 2. Hugging—Fiction. 3. Animals—Fiction.] • 1. Title. • PZ7.G2912Cu 2005 • [E]—dc22 • 2004006236 • Typography by Stephanie Bart-Horvath 1 2 3 4 5 6 7 8 9 10 • ❖ • First Published in the Netherlands by Clavis Editions, 2003 • First U.S. edition, 2005

THE
CUDDLE
BOOK

BY GUIDO VAN GENECHTEN

HarperCollinsPublishers

Everybody

likes a good cuddle.

Monkeys

cuddle

gently . . .

and
turtles
cuddle
slowly.

DUCKS cuddle

with their beaks . . .

and
elephants
cuddle
with
their
trunks.

For
kangaroos,
cuddling is easy
(because they are always so close) . . .

but for **crabs,**

cuddling is hard.

Cats cuddle playfully . . .

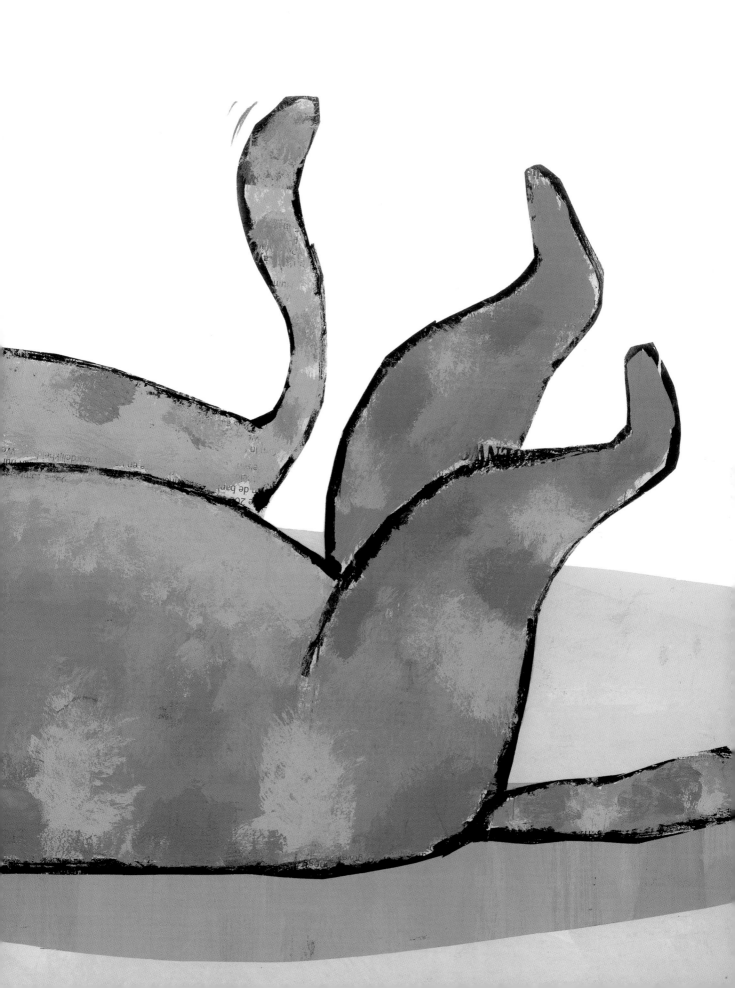

but porcupines

have to cuddle *very* carefully!

A **bear** hug is a very special cuddle.

But the
best cuddle
of all . . .

is **MOMMY'S** cuddle!